I Love You
Just Because You're You!

By Rochel Levy *Illustrated by Mary Chalmé Abadi*

Your picture here!

Dedication

To my kids,
who teach me what it's all about,
and make it all worth it!

R.L.

To Sheila, Yaakov and Judi:
We'll always love you,
head to toe.

M.A.

Esti forgot to close the door,
Got muddy footprints on the floor.

She climbed up to
the highest shelf,
To get a cookie
by herself.

She tried to pour
an ice-cold drink,
It fell and broke
inside the sink.

But Mommy kissed her on the head,
Hugged her tight and then she said,
"Keeping all the rules is tough,
To be a kid is hard enough!

"But boys and girls must listen well,
To what their parents show and tell.
There will be times when you'll forget,
And like today, you'll be upset."

"But…
I love you just because you're you,
And not for things you say or do.
We make mistakes, but you should know,
I'll always love you — head to toe."

Chaim disturbed
his father's rest,

Forgot to study
for his test.

Played baseball in
the living room,

Tried to swing
and broke the broom.

9

He drew
with markers
in his bed,

But, oops!
He ruined his
sheets instead.

Abba kissed him on his head,
Hugged him tight and then he said,
"Keeping all the rules is tough,
To be a kid is hard enough!

"You may be curious, you may be bored,
You may have thought you'd just explore.
Checking is the better way,
Ask, 'May I please? Is it okay?'"

"But...

I love you just because you're you,
And not for things you say or do.
We make mistakes, but you should know,
I'll always love you — head to toe."

Sara tried, but was not able,
To sit down at the Shabbos table.

She turned
the light on
by mistake,

And skipped
the *brachah*
on her cake.

She watched
her brothers,
all three boys,

But played
with Ari's
muktzeh toys.

Daddy kissed her on her head,
Hugged her tight and then he said,
"Keeping all the rules is tough,
To be a kid is hard enough!

"There are times we do things wrong,
And feel upset the whole day long.
But we must try with all our might,
Do what the Torah says is right."

"But...

I love you just because you're you,
And not for things you say or do.
We make mistakes, but you should know,
I'll always love you — head to toe."

Leah pushed
on line
at school,

Broke the
no-talking-
while-eating rule.

She took a toy,
but didn't say please,

And forgot the tissue
when she sneezed.

She borrowed, but
did not give back,

Refused to share
her recess snack.

Morah kissed her on her head,
Hugged her tight and then she said,
"Keeping all the rules is tough,
To be a kid is hard enough!

"Remember that the things you do,
Can hurt a friend that's next to you.
Adults and kids must stick to rules,
At home and work, in shuls and schools."

"But...

I love you just because you're you,
And not for things you say or do.
We make mistakes, but you should know,
I'll always love you — head to toe."

Dovi woke up
in a grumpy mood,

Began his day
by being rude.

When Zaidy asked him for a hug,
He answered with a grouchy shrug.

When Mother called,
he turned away,
Ignoring her
so he could play.

Now Tatty's home
and needs a hand,
But Dovi's lost
in Legoland.

28

His parents kissed him on his head,
Hugged him tight and then they said,
"Keeping all the rules is tough,
To be a kid is hard enough!

"We all feel crabby now and then,
Don't want to smile or help again.
We forget that Torah is our guide,
And end up feeling bad inside."

"But...

We love you just because you're you,
And not for things you say or do.
We make mistakes, but you should know,
We'll always love you — head to toe."

There is one Father up above,
Who cares for all His kids with love,
You and me and everyone,
Each a daughter or a son!

Always try to do what's right,
But remember in your bed each night,
That no matter what you said or did,
Hashem loves you 'cause you're His kid!

He loves you when you start your day,
And while you learn and work and play.
Hashem loves you the whole day through —
He loves you just because you're…